South Downs

river

W9-BAV-600

Button
found here

Ben's
house

Sky
found here

Chicken coop

Farmyard

Calf barn

Holly
found here

Jasmine's
house

Lucky
born here

To Roger Turner's farm →

2020

JUN

Jasmine Green Rescues
A Duckling Called Button

Read all the books in the
Jasmine Green Rescues series

Jasmine Green RESCUES

A Duckling Called Button

Helen Peters

illustrated by **Ellie Snowdon**

WALKER BOOKS

First U.S. edition 2020
First published by Nosy Crow (U.K.) 2017

Library of Congress Catalog Card Number pending
ISBN 978-1-5362-1025-5

20 21 22 23 24 25 LBM 10 9 8 7 6 5 4 3 2 1

Printed in Melrose Park, IL, U.S.A.

This book was typeset in Bembo.
The illustrations were done in pencil with a digital wash overlay.

Walker Books US
a division of
Candlewick Press
99 Dover Street
Somerville, Massachusetts 02144

www.walkerbooksus.com

A JUNIOR LIBRARY GUILD SELECTION

For my sister Mary
H. P.

For my mum, who taught me to fly
E. S.

1

Put That Down!

"Good girl, Truffle," said Jasmine, bending down to scratch her pig behind the ears. "Good girl."

Jasmine and her best friend, Tom, were walking Truffle around the edge of the biggest field on Oak Tree Farm, checking Jasmine's dad's flock of Southdown sheep. It was a lovely warm March morning. The sky was a beautiful pale blue, with high, fluffy clouds.

The sheep were due to lamb next month, and they had to be checked twice a day to make sure they were all right. Jasmine always took Truffle with her on these walks. She had rescued the pig from another farm, as a tiny newborn runt, and nursed her back to health. Now four months old, Truffle lived happily in the orchard next to the farmhouse, but she loved to go for walks with Jasmine.

"That sheep's stuck," said Tom, pointing toward the bottom of the field. A ewe lay upside down, arching her back and kicking her legs in the air, trying to get onto her feet.

The children walked quickly toward the sheep, Truffle trotting beside them.

"She must have rolled over to rub an itchy patch," said Jasmine. "She's too heavy in lamb to get up again, poor thing."

When they reached the stuck sheep, Jasmine said, "Sit, Truffle." Truffle sat obediently while Jasmine and Tom crouched beside the ewe.

"Let's get you back on your feet," Jasmine said. "We don't want a fox or a badger attacking you, do we?"

They placed their hands under the ewe's side and heaved her up. She scrambled to her feet and trotted off without a backward glance. Jasmine watched her happily. But Tom was frowning.

"There's a dog over there. Down by the river."

The far side of the meadow bordered the river. Trees and bushes grew along the banks. Some sheep had been grazing peacefully there, but now they started running across the field, baaing in panic.

Jasmine saw a flash of brown among the bushes.

"Off the leash, in a field full of sheep," she said. "It must be a stray. You run and get my dad. I'll stay here to chase it away if it tries to attack the ewes."

"Ugh," said Tom. "Look. I bet it's hers."

A girl in purple boots and a black coat with a fur-trimmed hood was walking along the public footpath that ran across the fields by the river. Somebody Jasmine and Tom knew all too well: Bella Bradley, the most annoying girl in their class.

Fury surged through Jasmine. She grabbed Truffle's leash and marched over to the girl.

"Bella Bradley! Is that your dog?"

Bella barely glanced at Jasmine. "Duh," she said. "Who else's dog would it be? I don't see anyone else around here."

"Well, you need to put it on a leash."

"Why should I?"

"Because these sheep are all in lamb. If your dog chases them, they could lose their lambs."

"My dog doesn't chase sheep. And you can't tell me what to do."

She strode off across the field.

Jasmine, boiling with rage, was about to retort when a tremendous squawking and beating of wings came from the direction of the river. She turned to see what was going on.

Bella's terrier shot out from the bushes. In its

mouth was a duck, flapping its wings and quacking frantically.

"Hey!" shouted Jasmine. "Put that down!"

She and Tom raced across the field after the dog, the duck clamped in its jaws. Tom picked up a clod of earth and hurled it at the terrier, but it missed.

When it reached the hedge, the dog dropped the duck and squeezed into the hedgerow. Jasmine and Tom fell to their knees beside the duck. It was a female mallard. Jasmine placed her hands on the soft, warm underbody.

There was no movement beneath her feathers. No heartbeat.

"She's dead," said Jasmine. "That dog killed her."

2
What If She Was Nesting?

Tom sprang to his feet. Jasmine had never seen him look so angry.

"Hey!" he yelled.

Bella carried on walking. "Rupert!" she called. "Rupert, come here!"

"Rupert?" scoffed Tom. "Awful name for a dog."

Jasmine got to her feet, cradling the duck in her arms. She and Tom ran across the field, stumbling over the rutted ground, Truffle trotting beside them.

"Hey!" shouted Tom again.

The dog still hadn't appeared, so Bella had to slow down. Tom and Jasmine caught up with her.

"Your dog," said Jasmine, standing in Bella's path, "just killed this duck."

Bella looked scornfully at the mallard's body.

"So?" she said. "It's just a duck. They're not exactly rare."

"What does that have to do with it?" said Jasmine. "What if she was nesting?"

"So what?" said Bella. She rounded on Tom. "Stop taking photos! Don't you know it's rude to take pictures without permission?"

"Don't you know it's rude to kill an animal without permission?" said Tom, pointing his phone at her face and clicking another shot.

"We'll report you," said Jasmine. "You won't get away with this."

"Oh, no," said Bella with an exaggerated fake shudder. "I'm so scared."

She gave them a contemptuous look and walked off. The terrier squeezed out of the

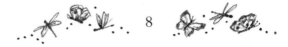

hedge and bounded over to her. Tom took several pictures of it.

"I hate her so much," said Jasmine.

"At least we can report her to the police," said Tom. "That'll give her a shock." He put the phone back in his pocket and stroked the duck. "Poor thing."

"We need to search the riverbank," said Jasmine. "In case she had a nest."

"Maybe there'll be ducklings," said Tom. "We could take them home and look after them."

"I think it's too early for ducklings," said Jasmine. "More likely to be eggs."

Tom's face lit up. "If it's eggs," he said, "we could put them in an incubator and hatch them."

Jasmine frowned. "I don't think we've got an incubator."

"Angela does," said Tom. "You know, my auntie. She hatches hens' eggs sometimes. I don't think that she's using it at the moment. I bet she'd lend it to us."

"We'll need to find the eggs quickly," said Jasmine, "if we're going to save them. If they go cold, they won't hatch."

They were nearly at the riverbank. Jasmine stopped and scanned the bushes.

"Was it here where the dog came out?"

Tom screwed up his face in thought. "I'm not sure."

"I think it was somewhere around here."

Tom bent down and picked up two small brown feathers and a piece of white fluff.

"Duck down and feathers," said Jasmine. "So it must have been around here."

They pushed their way through the bushes, following a trail of feathers, until they were almost at the river.

Then Jasmine saw it.

"Look!"

It sat in a hollow between the roots of a tree. One side had been destroyed, but what remained was half of the most beautiful nest

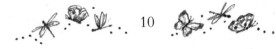

Jasmine had ever seen. It was made from leaves and grasses and lined with soft, fluffy duck down. On the downy lining nestled four perfect pale-green eggs.

Jasmine bent down and felt an egg. "They're still warm."

"Look at that," said Tom, pointing down to the riverbank.

A mess of smashed eggs lay on the ground. "The dog must have kicked them out of the nest."

Jasmine held the dead duck closer to her. Like all female mallards, her feathers were mostly shades of brown, with one beautiful inky-blue feather on her wing. "Poor, poor thing. All that work for nothing. They pluck the down from their own breasts to make that soft lining for the eggs."

"But it won't be for nothing, will it?" said Tom. "There's still four eggs. And we can hatch them in the incubator."

"If they're fertile," said Jasmine.

She handed the duck to Tom and scrambled down the riverbank, holding on to branches and tufts of grass to stop herself from slipping into the water.

"What are you doing?" called Tom.

"Seeing if they're fertile."

She reached the smashed eggs. Holding on to a low branch with one hand, she crouched down to inspect the yolks. Two were broken, but the other three were still intact. In the center of each was a little patch of red, with spidery veins coming out from it.

Jasmine turned to Tom. "They are fertile. If we get them into an incubator quickly, we could save them!"

"I'll phone Angela now," said Tom, "and see if she'll lend us her incubator." He took his phone from his pocket.

"Ask her if she can come over straightaway," said Jasmine. "Tell her it's an emergency."

She put an egg in each of her pockets and held out the other two to Tom. "Put these in your pockets. We need to keep them warm or the ducklings won't hatch."

 13

3

I'll Call the Rescue Center

It was while they were walking slowly back across the field with the eggs in their pockets that the tricky issue of parenthood occurred to Jasmine.

"You know ducklings become attached to the first moving thing they see?" she said.

"Do they?"

"It's called imprinting. I read about it. Usually it's their mom, obviously, but these ducklings don't have a mom. So they'll imprint on you or me, depending on which one of us they see first. So . . . who's going to have the incubator in their house?"

She paused and looked at Tom. "It should be you, really. It's your auntie who's lending us the incubator."

"Yes, but the eggs were on your farm."

"True. But they'd die without the incubator."

They walked on in silence for a minute. Then Tom said, "My mom would never let me have them. It took years to persuade her to let me have the guinea pigs. And our garden is tiny. They'd have a better life here."

Jasmine felt excitement surging through her. "Are you sure?"

"And your mom's a vet, so she'll know what to do if they get sick."

Jasmine felt a rush of gratitude toward her friend. "You can visit every day," she said, "and help look after them. They'll be ours jointly."

"Except they'd better imprint on you," said

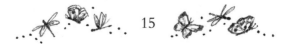

Tom. "Otherwise they'll be following me home all the time."

When they reached the farmyard, Jasmine took Truffle back to the orchard before they went into the house by the front door, pulling off their boots on the porch.

"Jas, is that you?" called her mom. "Where have you been all this time?"

She came into the hall and her eyes fell upon the dead duck in Jasmine's arms. "Oh, my goodness, what happened?"

Jasmine's words poured out in a torrent. "Oh, Mom, that horrible Bella Bradley from our class had her dog loose in the sheep field and we told her to put it on a leash but she refused, and he took this poor duck off her nest and killed her and we went and found the nest, and look."

She laid the dead duck on the hall table. Mom opened her mouth to protest and then shut it again. From each of her coat pockets Jasmine took a beautiful pale-green egg.

"There are four of them. Tom's got the others. There were five more, but the dog broke them. And Mom, they're fertile! So we need to get them into an incubator quickly."

"OK, Jasmine," said Mom, "calm down a minute. Come into the kitchen and we'll have a think. And let's get that dead duck off the table."

"Don't take her away. We're going to have a proper funeral and bury her in the garden, next to Blossom."

Blossom was Jasmine's pet hen. She had been killed by a fox last winter. The memory of it was still unbearably sad for Jasmine.

Mom was rummaging in the hall cupboard. "I'll put her in this shoebox for now. We need to think what to do about the eggs."

"They're still warm," said Jasmine, "but they'll need to go in an incubator soon, won't they?"

"It depends whether the duck had started incubating them yet. Was it just a red spot you saw, or was there any veining?"

"There were little spidery lines coming out of the spot."

"So she had started sitting. The ducklings are

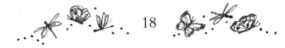 18

already growing. I'll phone the wildlife rescue center and we'll take them straight over there."

Jasmine looked at her in horror. "You can't take them away! They're ours."

"This is a specialist job, Jasmine. The wildlife rehabilitators do this kind of thing all the time and they're very good. And anyway, we don't have an incubator."

Jasmine glanced at Tom. "What if we did? Would you let us keep them?"

"Well, we don't, so there's no point discussing it. I'll phone them now."

Tom opened his mouth, but Jasmine shook her head at him.

"Why didn't you tell her we've got an incubator coming?" Tom whispered as they followed Mom to the kitchen.

"Because she might phone Angela and tell her not to bring it."

"But what if she takes the eggs away before Angela gets here?"

"We won't let her."

Jasmine's father was sitting at the kitchen table, eating a sandwich. Her fifteen-year-old sister, Ella, and five-year-old brother, Manu, were also having lunch. Ella was reading a book propped open on the table in front of her.

Dad raised his eyebrows when he saw the eggs.

"Where did you get those from?"

Jasmine and Tom told him. When they had finished, Dad looked thoughtful.

"This girl is in your class, did you say?"

He asked them for her name and address and typed them into his phone.

"Mallards and their nests are protected by law," he said. "It's an offense to damage or destroy them intentionally. And it's also an offense for a dog to be loose in a field of sheep. I'd have been within my rights to shoot it, if I'd seen it."

"I wouldn't want it shot," said Jasmine. "It's Bella's fault, not the dog's."

"It's the dog that could scare the sheep, though, and the dog that killed that duck." He stood up. "I'll call the police."

"And I'll call the rescue center," said Mom, "and let them know to expect a clutch of duck eggs in the next half hour."

Jasmine and Tom looked at each other in alarm.

"You don't have to phone them yet, do you?" asked Jasmine. "Why don't you wait for a bit?"

21

Please come soon, Angela, she thought. What was taking her so long?

"You said yourself, Jasmine, it's vital to get the eggs in an incubator as soon as possible," said Mom. "The sooner I take them to the rescue center, the better."

4
Give Me That Egg

"Should we put the eggs in the Aga?" Jasmine asked her mother. The Aga stove had four sections, each set at a different temperature. "Just in the warming oven?"

Anything to stop her from making that phone call.

Mom shook her head. "No, they might overheat, and that would kill the embryos. What you're doing right now — holding them in your hands — is the best thing. The warmth from your hands is probably about the same temperature as their mother's body. And—"

She was interrupted by a series of long, insistent rings on the doorbell that could only have come from one person.

Manu jumped up from his chair. His best friend, Ben, lived in the house at the end of the farm road. Like Tom, he spent as much of his time at the farm as he possibly could. And he always signaled his arrival in the same way.

"You finish your lunch, Manu," said Mom. "I'll let Ben in."

"But I've finished."

"You certainly have not. You need to eat those vegetables before you leave the table."

She left the room.

"I need to use the bathroom," said Tom. "Where shall I put the eggs?"

Ella looked up from her book. "I'll hold them," she said.

"Thanks, Ella," said Jasmine, amazed. Her sister was usually too absorbed in reading or studying to think about anything else.

"It's fine. I can read while I'm holding them. Give them here, Tom."

"Be really careful," said Jasmine. "If they crack, they won't hatch."

As Ella sat back down with an egg in each hand, Mom brought Ben into the kitchen.

"Take a seat, Ben," she said. "Manu's just finishing his lunch."

"Thank you, Dr. Singh," said Ben, sitting in the chair opposite Manu.

Ben was always extremely polite to adults. That was how he got away with misbehaving so much.

"I'm glad you're better," said Mom. "It can't have been fun, having pneumonia. Especially having to stay in the hospital."

Ben's eyes lit up. "The hospital was so fun. I had this really cool bed with a button you could press to make it go up and down. Only I pressed it so much the button broke. But then a man came and fixed it. And I had my own TV on the wall and I could watch it all day long."

Mom smiled. "Oh, well, that's great that you liked it."

"The only thing I didn't like was when my sister came to visit."

"Why, what did she do?"

"She blocked my view of the TV."

Mom laughed and went to unplug her phone from its charger on the dresser. As soon as her back was turned, Manu pushed his plate of carrot sticks and cherry tomatoes across the table to Ben, who stuffed them all in his mouth at once and slid the plate back to Manu.

"Finished," said Manu. "Can we go and play now?"

"Off you go, then," said Mom. "Right, I need to make this phone call."

She picked up her phone and left the room.

"Thank you, Dr. Singh," said Ben through a mouthful of vegetables.

As he stood up, Ben suddenly noticed what Jasmine and Ella held in their hands.

"Why are you holding eggs? Is it a game?"

Jasmine explained everything.

"So there's ducklings already growing in them?" said Ben. "That's so cool! Let's crack one open and see."

"Don't be mean," said Jasmine. "You'd kill the duckling."

"I'd only break one. You'd still get three ducklings."

Jasmine gave him her most withering stare.

"She's such a spoilsport," said Manu. "Come on, let's go."

"We could sit on the eggs and hatch them!" said Ben.

Jasmine snorted.

"They wouldn't break," he said.

"Of course they'd break."

"No, they wouldn't," said Manu. "We did this science experiment at school. If you stand an egg with the pointed end facing up, it won't break, even if you step on it. So we can definitely sit on

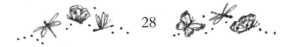

them. And then they'll hatch underneath us. Give me that egg, Ella."

"Huh?" said Ella vaguely, glancing up from her book.

"No!" shouted Jasmine.

But Manu held out his hand, and Ella, who had obviously been too absorbed in her book to listen to the conversation, let him take it.

"Give that back!" yelled Jasmine. "Don't you dare sit on it!"

She rushed around the table, but she had an egg in each hand and, as she desperately looked around for a safe place to put them, Manu positioned the egg on the floor with the pointed end facing up and plunked himself down on top of it.

A cracking, crunching sound came from underneath him.

"Oops," said Ben.

"You *monster*!" screamed Jasmine. "You horrible monster! I hate you!"

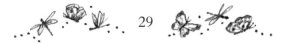

Still clutching her eggs, she swung out her leg and kicked her brother.

"Get off me!" he shouted, scrambling to his feet. "It's not my fault!"

"You killed the duckling!" shouted Jasmine, tears of anger in her eyes at the sight of the crushed, slippery mess on the floor. "I told you not to do it. I *told* you."

"How was I supposed to know it wouldn't work?" protested Manu. "It worked in the experiment. There must have been something wrong with that egg. I bet it was bad."

Jasmine aimed another kick at him. Manu ran out of the room, down the corridor, and into the hall. Jasmine chased after him.

Tom emerged from the downstairs bathroom, looking horrified. "Stop it!" he shouted. "You'll break the eggs!"

"What on *earth* is going on?" asked Mom, appearing from the living room with her phone in her hand.

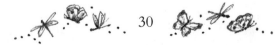

Jasmine and Manu both shouted at once.

"It's him! He killed a duckling!"

"It's her! She kicked me! And I didn't do anything!"

The doorbell rang.

"Stay right there, both of you," said Mom. "Don't move an inch and don't say a word."

"Murderer," muttered Jasmine to Manu.

Mom opened the front door. On the step stood a tall woman with a border collie at her side, wagging his feathery tail. The woman was holding a round plastic container the size of a cake tin, with

a cord and a plug. It had a yellow base, clear sides, and a black lid with buttons and a digital display.

"Hello," said Mom. "Can I help you?" She sounded puzzled.

The woman smiled. "Hello. You must be Jasmine's mom. I'm Angela. Tom's auntie."

"Oh, nice to meet you. Have you come to pick up Tom? He's right here."

"No, I'm not here for Tom," said Angela. "I've brought that incubator you wanted to borrow."

5
What Incubator?

"I'm sorry?" said Mom. "What incubator?"

She turned at the sound of Dad's footsteps on the stairs.

"Michael, did you ask Tom's aunt to bring over an incubator?"

Dad looked bemused. "Did I what?"

"No, it was Tom who phoned," said Angela. "He said you had some duck eggs that needed incubating."

Tom sidled closer to Jasmine.

Before her parents had a chance to speak, Jasmine said, "Please let us hatch them. We'll learn all about it. You know I can look after hens, and I've looked after Truffle, haven't I?"

"You've done a great job with Truffle," said Dad. "Nobody could have looked after her better."

Jasmine turned to her mother. "Please, Mom? It will be so lovely to have ducklings. And it will be great experience for when we have our rescue center."

Jasmine and Tom were determined to run an animal rescue center when they grew up. They were already planning the details.

Mom turned to Angela. "I'm so sorry about all this. Please come in."

"Oh, I won't, thank you. Not with Jake."

Mom opened the door wider. "What a lovely dog. Bring him in, too."

"Sit, Jake," said Angela as she walked into the hall. Jake sat immediately, swishing his tail across the carpet, looking adoringly at his owner.

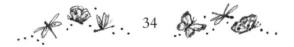

"As you might have gathered," Mom said, "this has come as a bit of a surprise. I was just about to take the eggs to a rescue center. And judging by Jasmine's behavior since she brought them home, I'm really not sure she's mature enough to look after them. Honestly, Jasmine. Racing around screaming with the eggs in your hands, for goodness' sake."

"It wasn't Jasmine's fault," said Ella.

Everyone turned to look at her. She stood in the doorway, her book in her hand. "Manu took one of the eggs I was holding and sat on it."

"I was trying to hatch it," said Manu. "They're not supposed to break."

Dad looked at Manu as though he had just landed from another planet.

"Why on *earth* would you do that?"

Mom's phone beeped. She read the message and frowned. "Sorry, Angela. I'm on call this weekend. I'm going to have to go. And I'm afraid I really don't know what to do about this egg business.

We're busy enough without hatching ducklings."

"But we'll do it all," said Jasmine. "You won't have to do anything."

"Angela will help us set up the incubator," said Tom. He turned to his aunt. "Won't you?"

"And Tom knows a lot already," said Jasmine. "He's helped Angela before."

"I'm happy to help," Angela said to Mom.

Mom gave a helpless sort of shrug. "Michael?"

Dad looked thoughtful. "It would be a good thing for Jasmine to learn. And there's not much that beats seeing a duckling hatch from an egg."

Mom sighed and picked up her car keys. "Fine. But you need to do the work, Jasmine. I really haven't got the time."

Behind Mom's back, Tom and Jasmine exchanged delighted grins. They were going to have their very own ducklings!

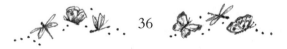

"The first thing to do," said Angela once Mom had left, "is to plug this in and get it up to the right temperature. Which room are you planning to keep it in?"

"My bedroom," said Jasmine. "Then I can look after the eggs and watch the ducklings hatch."

"That should be fine," said Angela, "as long as you make sure you keep the room at roughly the same temperature the whole time."

Jasmine took everything off the low table by her bed to make room for the incubator. Her cats, Toffee and Marmite, were curled up asleep on her duvet, their paws intertwined. They opened

their eyes lazily as Jasmine murmured to them and stroked their silky fur.

"The temperature's on the display there," said Angela when Jasmine had switched the incubator on. "Once it gets to 99.5 degrees, you can put the eggs in. And while we're waiting, you can wash them. I'll get the solution from the car."

"Why do we need to wash them?" Jasmine asked.

"Germs can pass through the shell," said Tom. "So you wash them with this special egg-cleaning solution."

Jasmine looked at her grubby hands, alarmed. "But we've been holding them all this time. What if germs have already gotten in?"

"I'm sure they'll be fine," said Angela. "Just remember to wash your hands before handling them from now on."

Once they had washed the eggs, Tom suggested candling them while they waited for the incubator to get to the right temperature.

"It's really cool," he said. "You shine a flashlight

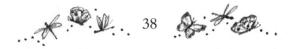

through the shell and you can see if there's a duckling growing inside."

Jasmine fetched her flashlight from its hook by the back door. "Will this work?"

Angela switched it on. "Perfect. Close the curtains, Jasmine. The darker it is, the better we'll see. And could you fetch me a pencil? With a soft lead, if possible."

"Why do we need a pencil?" asked Jasmine, inspecting the random assortment in the jam jar on her windowsill, trying to find one with an unbroken lead.

"To number the eggs," said Tom, "so we can tell them apart."

"And you'll have to turn them by hand several times a day," said Angela, "because duck eggs are too big for the automatic turning tray to work. So if there's a number on one side of the egg, you'll be able to see that you've turned them all. Turning them is really important. It means the ducklings can move around in the egg white and don't get stuck to one side of the shell."

Jasmine picked up an egg and carefully wrote a number one on it. Then she handed it to Angela, who held it up and shone the flashlight beam through the back of the shell. The egg glowed golden red.

"Wow," said Jasmine. "It looks like Mars. Only egg-shaped."

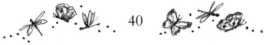

It had pipped! The first duckling was breaking out of its shell!

"Hello, little duckling," whispered Jasmine. "Are you all right in there? I can't wait to see you."

She scrutinized the other egg, but it was still intact. Not the tiniest little crack. She hoped it was all right.

She ran down to the kitchen, where Mom was stirring a pan of porridge on the Aga stove.

"Mom, Egg One has pipped!"

Mom turned and smiled at her. "Oh, that's great news. Well done, Jasmine."

"So I need the day off from school. Will you call the office?"

Mom laughed. "You can't have the day off from school because you might have eggs hatching."

Jasmine stared at her mother, aghast.

"Of *course* I need the day off. It's the most important day of my life. I bet you had the day off from work when your babies were born."

"That's a little bit different."

"I don't see how."

Mom sighed. "Jasmine, you're not actually giving birth to these ducklings. And the hatching process can take a long time, you know that, and it needs to happen without interference. And even after they've hatched, they have to stay in the incubator for twenty-four hours to dry out and to fluff up their down. So you really don't need the day off from school."

"But I *have* to be there. If I'm not the first moving thing they see, how will they recognize me as their mother? If you or Dad see them before me, they'll imprint on you instead, and that would be so unfair."

"Believe me, Jasmine," said Mom, "the last thing I need is a pair of ducklings following me around. Dad and I won't even go into the room. We'll just peep in every now and then. We'll make sure you're the first moving thing your ducklings see. I promise."

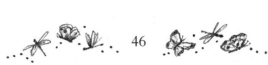

School seemed to go on forever that day. Jasmine was fizzing with excitement so much that she couldn't stop squirming in her seat.

"Do you need to use the restroom?" asked Bella Bradley, pausing in the act of brushing her long blond hair for the trillionth time. "Why don't you just go?"

Jasmine ignored her. She hadn't spoken to Bella since the duck incident. If she had to share a table with the girl she loathed more than anyone else in the world, the only way to make it bearable was to pretend that Bella didn't exist.

"Bella Bradley," said Mr. Hampton, "if I see that hairbrush one more time today, I will be confiscating it."

By half past two, Jasmine was bubbling with anticipation and impatience so much that she actually fell off her chair. Mr. Hampton didn't see her sprawled between the tables and accidentally stepped on her hand before she could get to her feet.

 47

"What the—" he exclaimed, looking down with startled eyes. "Jasmine! What on earth are you doing?"

"Freak," whispered Bella as Jasmine scrambled back into her seat, rubbing her squished hand.

Jasmine ignored her.

She knew the police had been to Bella's house after her dog had killed the duck. The police-woman had phoned Dad and told him.

"They gave her a stern warning," Dad said, "to keep her dog on a leash in any field containing livestock in the future."

"Is that all? A warning? She should be put in prison."

"They can't prove she intentionally let her dog kill the duck," Dad had said, "so there's nothing more they can do. I think she was pretty shocked, though, to have the police turn up on her doorstep. And they warned her that if I'd seen the dog, I'd have been within my rights to shoot it on the spot. So I don't think she'll be letting it run free again."

"That's not good enough, though," said Jasmine. "These ducklings will be orphans because of her, and she gets away without any punishment at all. It's not fair."

Dad had sighed. "Sometimes, Jas, life isn't fair."

That was certainly true, Jasmine thought now. There were twenty-nine other people in her class. In a fair world, she would not have been forced to spend six hours a day sitting next to Bella Bradley.

Ten minutes before the end of school, Mr. Hampton asked the class to empty their desk drawers for break. Bella opened her drawer and placed on the table seven pots of lip gloss, three pocket mirrors, and four hairbrushes. "What are you going to do for your project?" she asked Jasmine.

Jasmine shrugged.

Mr. Hampton had assigned them a vacation project. They had to make something from things they had found in the world around them, write an account of how they made it, and bring it in to show the class on the first day of the quarter.

"I'm going to make my own beauty products," said Bella. "With natural ingredients. It's going to be amazing. I'll sell the recipes to a massive beauty company, and I'll be a millionaire."

Jasmine ignored her. She emptied out the contents of her drawer, which consisted of an assortment of candy wrappers, a copy of her favorite magazine, *Practical Pigs,* and several balls of crumpled-up paper torn from exercise books, which were the notes that she and Tom smuggled to each other during lessons.

"Don't put any of your stuff on my side," said Bella, pushing a scrap of paper away and indicating an invisible line down the middle of the table. "Can't you see I'm trying to keep it tidy?"

Jasmine swept all her things into her bag. Then she turned her chair upside down on the table and stood behind it, trying to catch the teacher's eye so he would let her out.

Tom was also standing behind his chair. She caught his eye and grinned. All the annoyances of school melted away. She was about to have two beautiful ducklings of her very own.

7
I Hope They're All Right

As soon as Jasmine and Tom got to the farmhouse, they raced up to Jasmine's room. "I have to go in first," said Jasmine. "If they've hatched, I have to be the first moving thing they see."

She peered into the incubator. Egg One hadn't changed since the morning. And Egg Two was still intact.

"I hope they're all right," Jasmine said. "It's a long time without anything happening."

"Let's stay and watch," said Tom. "It would be so cool to see one hatch."

They sat on Jasmine's bed, scrutinizing the eggs for signs of life. But nothing happened. After what seemed like a very long time, the back door opened and they heard Manu and Ben talking. Dad called up the stairs. "Jasmine, there's a package here for you."

Jasmine jumped up. "Yay! I thought they weren't going to arrive in time." She turned to the incubator. "You keep trying to break out, little ones. We'll be back very soon."

"But what if they hatch when we're not here?"

"I don't think they will. Anyway, we'll only be a minute."

They ran downstairs. Dad was standing in the kitchen in his socks, warming his hands at the big Aga stove that gave off heat all day and all night. Manu and Ben sat at the table, drinking milk and eating cookies.

"How are the eggs?" asked Dad, who hadn't been around at breakfast time.

"Egg One pipped this morning," said Jasmine.

"Oh, good. How eggciting."

Jasmine groaned. "That is a terrible joke. Is that my package?"

Dad handed her a cardboard box. "It's addressed to you."

Jasmine ripped off the tape, opened the box,

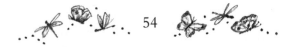

and rummaged through the bubble wrap. She pulled out a little bag.

"Elastic bands?" said Ben. "Why did you buy elastic bands on the internet? You can get those in town."

"They're not normal elastic bands," said Jasmine. "They're leg bands for the ducklings." She tore the bag open and shook the bands out on the kitchen table. "I ordered a different color for each of them, and eight different sizes in each color, so I can change them as they grow."

"An eggcellent idea," said Dad. "Sorry, Jas."

"Have you picked names for them?" asked Ben.

"I've thought of some," said Jasmine, "but I'm going to wait until they're born to see if they suit them."

"Dave," said Manu. "You've got to call one Dave."

"Alan," said Ben.

"Keith."

"Those are so normal," said Jasmine, who was

pulling more bubble wrap out of the box. "And they're all boys' names. The ducklings might be girls."

"When can you actually tell if they're ducks or drakes?" asked Tom.

"Not until they're four or five weeks old," said Jasmine, "when they start quacking. Females quack much louder than males."

She pulled out a clear plastic dome with a yellow tray at the bottom, wider than the dome.

"What's that?" asked Ben.

"It's a duckling drinker. You put the water in the top of the dome and it goes into the tray for

the ducklings to drink, but because the dome's in the middle of the tray, they can't get in it to swim."

"Why don't you want them to swim?"

"If they're not hatched by their mother, they can't swim for the first few weeks."

"Why? Does their mom give them swimming lessons?" asked Manu.

Ben's face lit up. "We could give them swimming lessons! Can we take them to the pool? That would be so cool. We could get them little mini life jackets."

"It's not about teaching them to swim," said Jasmine. "Ducks have oil glands so they can oil their feathers to make themselves waterproof, but ducklings' oil glands don't work until they're a few weeks old. So the mother duck spreads her oil on the ducklings. But these ones don't have a mother, so their feathers won't be waterproof until their oil glands start working."

"Why don't *we* oil the ducklings?" said Ben. "It

57

would be a cool experiment. We could try all different oils to see which worked best. Sunflower oil, olive oil . . ."

"Tractor oil," said Manu.

"And leave the other one without any oil on, just to see what happens."

"I can tell you what would happen," said Jasmine. "It would get waterlogged and drown."

"How do you know, though?" said Manu. "I bet no one's ever tried it."

"Maybe because no one wants their ducklings to drown."

"How was the last day of the quarter, Jasmine?" asked Dad.

"Same as usual," said Jasmine, peeling the label off the plastic dome on the drinker.

"Except for George setting fire to the toilets," said Tom.

Jasmine laughed. "That was funny."

"George did what?" asked Dad.

"He stuffed all the toilet paper down one of

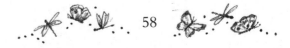

the toilets and set fire to it with his lighter," said Jasmine.

"With his *what*?"

"This lighter he brought into school," said Tom. "He said he found it on the sidewalk. The fire alarm went off and we all had to stand in the playground for hours, freezing to death."

"I thought it would be Manu and Ben," said Jasmine. "I was really relieved when we found out it was George."

Manu and Ben looked outraged. "That is so unfair," said Manu. "We only set the fire alarm off once."

"And it wasn't our fault," said Ben. "Alfie pushed us into it."

"Well, I hope George isn't still wandering around with a lighter," said Dad.

"No, Mrs. Murphy took it from him," said Tom. "She said it wasn't an appropriate thing to bring into school. And his mom had to come and get him."

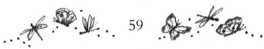

"Poor woman," said Dad.

"Oh, and we have to do a vacation project," said Jasmine. "To make something from things we've found in nature. Bella Bradley's making beauty products."

Manu made a face. "She would."

"I'm going to make things out of wood," said Tom. Much to his mom's horror, his grandparents had given him a real tool set for Christmas.

"I can't think of anything to do," said Jasmine.

"You should make a monster," said Ben, "out of Manu's skull-and-bone collection."

"That would be so cool," said Manu. "You could use the fox's head and then put the legs of four different animals on it."

"No, five legs," said Ben, "from five different animals."

"And call it the Beast of Oak Tree Farm."

"It should be a two-headed monster," said Ben. "You could put the badger's head on the other end."

"If you think I'm going near any of those

disgusting skulls," said Jasmine, "that you don't even wash before you put in your bedroom—"

"I do wash them."

"Not properly."

"Oh, by the way," said Dad, "Angela phoned. She knows you want to board animals to fund your rescue center. She's away during spring vacation and her dog sitter isn't around. She wondered if you'd like to watch Jake."

"For a whole week? I'd love to!"

"You'd have to keep him on a leash around the sheep."

"Of course I will."

"Come on," said Tom, "let's go and check the eggs. I really want one to hatch while I'm here."

"Can't you just crack the shell open and get it out?" said Ben.

"No!" said Jasmine. "Not unless nothing's happened for ages and ages. It's a really big thing for them to get hatched. You have to let them do it in their own time."

They ran upstairs again and stared into the incubator.

"Nothing different," said Tom. "Not even one more tiny crack."

"Let's do some designs for the rescue center while we wait," said Jasmine.

She got out the big pad of art paper she had been given for Christmas and they lay sprawled on the rug, drawing maps of the animal rescue center and boarding place they were going to run

when they were grown up. Every few minutes, they got up to look at the eggs, but there was no change. Tom reluctantly left at half past five, and still nothing had happened.

"Call me as soon as one hatches," he said to Jasmine.

"I will."

By the time Mom got home at six, the day already felt like the longest of Jasmine's life.

"The eggs are probably bad," Manu said helpfully.

"Don't be silly," said Jasmine. "How can they be bad if a duckling is cracking open the shell?"

"That's the badness coming out. Soon they'll explode. That's what rotten eggs do."

"Shut up, Manu," said Jasmine. "You know nothing. Anyway, me and Mom have been candling them. We know there are ducklings in them."

"If they explode, they really stink," Manu said hopefully.

Right after dinner, Jasmine ran back to her room. And what she saw when she looked in the incubator made her gasp with horror.

There was a duckling on the incubator floor. It was wet and slimy, as ducklings are when they first hatch. But it wasn't cheeping. Its eyes were shut. And it was completely still.

For a few seconds, Jasmine stood over the incubator, frozen to the spot, her heart thudding against her ribs. Then she unfroze, rushed out of her room, and hurtled down the stairs. She

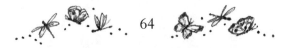

missed her footing on the bottom step and crashed onto the hall floor.

Mom came running into the hall.

"Jasmine! Are you all right?"

Jasmine scrambled to her feet. "There's a duckling," she sobbed, grabbing her mother's hand and dragging her to the stairs. "And I think it's dead."

Mom followed Jasmine to her room. She peered into the incubator. Then she lifted

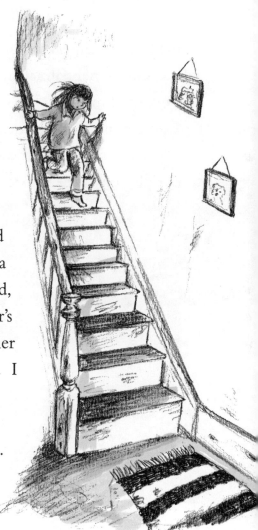

the lid, gently picked up the tiny duckling, and replaced the lid.

She laid her fingers softly on the little creature's side as it lay in her palm. Jasmine stood beside her, holding her breath.

After a minute, Mom turned to Jasmine.

"I'm really sorry, sweetheart," she said, "but you were right. This little one is dead."

8
Sometimes These Things Happen

It was nearly midnight when Jasmine finally cried herself to sleep. She had put the little duckling, whom she had named Petal, in a box that she had lined with fabric, and surrounded it with buttercups and daisies. They had buried Petal in the garden, next to its mother. At the funeral, Ella read a sad poem about death in springtime.

Jasmine was inconsolable. As well as feeling desperately sorry for the poor little duckling that would never see the world, she was also choked with guilt. She was their mother. It was her job to keep them safe. And she had failed. She had let her duckling die. She hadn't even been there when the poor little thing had hatched. She had been downstairs, eating her dinner. How long had that tiny motherless creature suffered on its own?

"It didn't suffer," said Mom. "There was nothing more you could have done, Jasmine. This sometimes happens, I'm afraid. Not all eggs produce live ducklings."

But Jasmine was racked with guilt. Why had the duckling died? Had she damaged it when she had chased after Manu with the eggs in her hands? Had it been too long before the eggs went into the incubator? Had she done something wrong during the incubation period?

"We'll never know," said Mom. "You looked after those eggs as well as you possibly could, Jasmine. It's very sad, but sometimes these things happen."

When she went back to her room after the

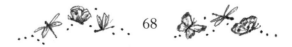

funeral, Egg Two had pipped. But this time, Jasmine felt no excitement at all. Because her worst worry of all was so terrible that she couldn't even say it out loud.

If there had been something wrong with Petal, was there something wrong with this one, too?

Would both ducklings be born dead?

Nothing anybody said could give her the slightest comfort. Both her ducklings were going to die, and it was all her fault. She wouldn't be able to bear it.

When she woke on Saturday morning, her first thought was for her dead duckling. She buried her head in her pillow. The thought of looking into the incubator terrified her. She didn't have the courage to face it.

Gradually, she became aware of a high-pitched squeaking noise. Sunk in misery, she didn't take much notice. Then, suddenly, her stomach did a somersault. She sat bolt upright and stared into the incubator.

There was no duckling. The egg was still whole. But that noise was definitely coming from the incubator.

It was the sound of a duckling, cheeping inside its egg.

"Oh!" she gasped. "Oh, you're talking!"

She scrambled out of bed and looked through the misty plastic dome into the incubator. And what she saw made her break out into a big smile.

The duckling in Egg Two had made a breathing hole. Tiny feathers stuck out of the hole. The feathers were moving as the duckling breathed. And the duckling was cheeping, loud and strong.

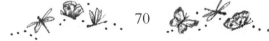

That must be a good sign, surely?

But what if Petal had cheeped like that, too, right before it died?

"I'm not going to leave you," she told her egg. "Not for one second. Not until you're safely hatched."

Should she wake Mom?

If nothing has happened by eight o'clock, Jasmine thought, *I'll wake her. Even though she wanted to sleep in this morning, she'll understand it's important.*

Wait a minute. What was that?

Jasmine squinted into the incubator.

Another tiny crack had appeared beside the breathing hole.

Something poked through the crack. A bill! A shiny little black duckling bill had pecked a hole through the eggshell. And it was cheeping loudly.

Jasmine kept her eyes fixed on the egg. She held her breath.

The bill disappeared inside the shell again.

Why had it gone back inside? Was something wrong?

The egg wobbled on the incubator tray.

Suddenly, a crack appeared right across the wide end of the shell. The bill poked out again. After a few seconds, it withdrew into the shell. It started to cheep again. The crack widened and Jasmine saw the duckling's wet downy feathers, yellow and brown, moving up and down as the duckling breathed, too.

Jasmine forced herself to breathe, too. The duckling breathed much faster than she did.

For several minutes, she stayed completely still, watching the feathers moving up and down. Every now and then the duckling cheeped for a few seconds.

Suddenly, the egg wobbled violently on the tray. The top lifted off as though it was hinged, and from underneath the eggshell appeared the little wet face of a tiny duckling. Its shiny round black eyes looked straight at Jasmine.

Jasmine felt as though she was about to burst with love and pride. She smiled through the incubator dome at the bedraggled little creature. "Hello, little duckling," she whispered. "Welcome to the world."

The duckling cheeped loudly. Jasmine's smile widened.

"You're saying hello, aren't you? I'm Jasmine. I'm going to be your mother."

The duckling kicked its legs. Its feet seemed to be stuck in the shell. Finally, it struggled out.

"No wonder they were stuck," Jasmine said, looking at the big webbed feet. "They're massive!"

The duckling lay curled on its side, breathing hard.

"You're all squished up, aren't you, like you were in the shell. You'll straighten out in a minute. I imagine you're gathering your strength."

As though it had understood her words, the duckling staggered to its feet. Bits of shell were stuck to its head. Jasmine smiled.

"Well done, little one. You're strong, aren't you? Strong and determined."

The duckling lifted its head and looked straight at her. It looked amused and intelligent and curious.

"You understand everything, don't you?" said Jasmine, looking back into that shiny round eye. "You're such a clever duckling."

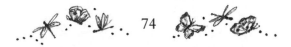

A surge of happiness overwhelmed her. She hadn't killed both her ducklings, after all. This one was alive and well and strong.

"You were just a tiny red blob in an egg when I found you," she said. "And look what you've grown into."

She considered for a minute, looking at the little creature regarding her from the incubator.

"I'm going to call you Button. I have a feeling you're a boy. I don't know why, but you seem like a boy to me. And if you turn out to be a girl, then Button will still be a cute name."

Button gave a series of piercing cheeps.

"Good boy," said Jasmine. "You like your name, don't you?"

She must call Tom, she thought. She had sobbed on the phone to him last night after Petal had died. He would have been worrying all this time.

She looked at her alarm clock. It was twenty past seven.

"I'll be back in a second," she told the duckling.

She ran downstairs, grabbed the cordless phone from the living room, and raced back up to the incubator. She dialed Tom's house number. There was no point calling his cell phone because he wasn't allowed to have it in his bedroom.

Luckily, it was Tom himself who answered.

"I knew it would be you," he said as soon as Jasmine said hello. "What's happening?"

"Oh, Tom, there's a beautiful, live, healthy duckling. He's called Button. He's just hatched. I'm sorry I didn't phone before, but it all happened so fast."

"I'm coming right now," he said. "I'll just tell Mom."

He arrived ten minutes later, red-cheeked and out of breath. They raced up to Jasmine's room. Button waddled across the incubator toward them, cheeping excitedly.

"Oh my goodness," said Tom. "He's so cute."

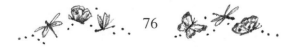

"He's the cutest duckling ever."

"He's amazing. I can't believe he knows you already."

Jasmine stared at him. "Do you think he does? How can you tell?"

"Of course he does. He ran over to greet you as soon as he heard your voice. And see the way he's looking at you. It's like he's smiling."

A wave of happiness washed over Jasmine. "He is, isn't he? He's really smiling."

Mom's voice came from the doorway. "Is anything happening?"

"Oh, Mom," said Jasmine, running to the door and pulling her mother across the room. "Look, the duckling has hatched! He's called Button."

Mom gazed into the incubator. "Oh, Jasmine, he's perfect."

"I wish I could hold him," said Jasmine, looking longingly at the wet little duckling waddling around the incubator.

"I know," said Mom, "but he needs to stay in there until his down has fluffed up. He could catch a chill if you take him out too early. It won't be long, and then you'll have a lovely fluffy duckling you can hold in your hands." She gave Jasmine a hug. "I'm so pleased for you. It's lovely to see you happy again."

"I'll never forget Petal, though."

"I know you won't. Now, I'm going to make breakfast. Tom, what would you like? Jas usually has a kati roll filled with eggs on Saturdays."

Jasmine made a face. She glanced at Tom, whose excitement had also faded at the mention of eggs.

"Could we have the kati rolls another way?" asked Jasmine. "It's just . . . I don't really feel like eating eggs this morning."

9
He'll Be So Lonely

"Are you coming to the talent show?" Manu asked Mom as they were having breakfast on the following Saturday.

"The school talent show? I thought you weren't entering."

"I am now."

Mom looked at Manu curiously. "Really? I thought you hated being onstage. You kept your eyes screwed shut the whole way through the Christmas show."

"Who are you entering with?" asked Jasmine.

"Ben and Noah."

"Are you singing?" Mom asked.

"No."

"Dancing?"

"Ugh, no."

"So what are you doing?"

"Fire eating," said Manu.

Mom roared with laughter. "Fire eating?"

"Yes."

"How can you do that?" asked Jasmine. "You'll set yourselves on fire."

"Noah says his mom's got this stuff you put in your mouth and the fire doesn't burn you. We're going to practice at his house."

"Does Miss Taplin know what you're planning?" asked Mom.

"We haven't told her yet."

"Well, I'll be interested to hear what she says when you do. Oh, Jasmine, take that duckling off the table. How many times have I told you not

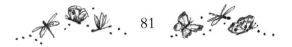

81

to let him drink from your
glass?"

"But he loves it," said
Jasmine.

"That's not the point."

Button took his bill out of Jasmine's glass and
shook himself dry, spraying water all over her
plate. He waddled to the edge of the table and
plopped onto Jasmine's lap. Jasmine stroked her
duckling's fluffy yellow down with its brown
mallard markings. She still couldn't get over how
soft and light he was.

"Mom, does he have to go to the barn today?
He'll be so lonely."

"He can't stay in the house forever, Jasmine.
He needs to get used to being outside. You can
still spend all day with him, just like you do now.
And when you go back to school, he can go in
with the chickens."

"He might not like the chickens. I think he
likes people better."

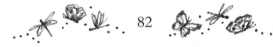

"He likes the duck in the mirror," said Manu. "And his stuffed animal."

Button's home for the first week of his life had been a cardboard box beside Jasmine's bed. Following the advice she had read about looking after a single duckling, Jasmine had given him a soft toy to snuggle up with and taped a mirror to the side of the box so Button had another duck to look at and talk to. Button seemed to like the duck in the mirror, and enjoyed cheeping at it and watching it cheep back at him. But actually he spent almost all his time with Jasmine. He followed her around the house, sat on her lap at mealtimes, and snuggled in her coat pocket when she took Truffle for walks. He only went into his box at night.

Jasmine had wanted Button to sleep on her pillow, but her parents had been horrified at the idea.

"Ducks are incredibly messy, and you can't house-train them," said Mom. "It's quite enough that he's in the house all day."

On Button's first night in the box, Jasmine

had sneaked him out and let him sleep beside her. But the state of her pillow in the morning had proved the truth of Mom's words, and even Jasmine decided it was probably a good thing if Button spent his nights in the box.

Now the duckling nibbled affectionately at Jasmine's hand as she stroked his down.

"You won't be lonely outside, I promise," she said. "I'm going to spend every day with you."

She picked him up, rose from her chair, and put her cereal bowl in the dishwasher.

"See you later," she said to Mom. "I'm going to take him to the lambing barn."

Most of the sheep had lambed by now, and the older lambs had already gone out to the field with their mothers. Dad had divided the barn into pens of different sizes. In the largest pen were the sheep with young lambs that weren't quite strong enough to go out to the field yet. In the second-largest one were the sheep who were still waiting to lamb. And in the row of small individual pens were the sheep with newborn lambs who needed an eye kept on them.

The pen at the far end of this row was different, though. Like the others, it was made of metal rails connected together, but this one also had chicken wire around the rails.

Jasmine set Button's box down outside the pen, climbed over the rails, and leaned back to lift the box inside. She placed it carefully on the fresh bed of chopped straw with which she had covered the floor, under the heat lamp that Dad had strung above the pen. She opened the flaps, and the little duckling ran, cheeping in greeting, to the edge of the box. She scooped him into her palm. He looked at her with his bright round eyes.

"It's a big day for you, Button. You're going to live in the barn now. You've got a whole lovely pen of your own to play in."

A sudden movement on the far side of the barn caught Jasmine's eye. She looked up to see a big gray rat scuttling into a gap between two bales. She shuddered. It was a good thing they had put chicken wire all around Button's pen, she

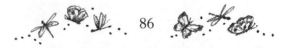

thought, scanning the wire to check there weren't any gaps. It wouldn't take a very big hole for a rat to squeeze through. Button, clumsy and unable to fly yet, would be easy prey. She would have to cover the top of the pen with netting, too, when she wasn't with him.

"What am I going to do for my project, Button?" Jasmine asked her duckling, stroking his down.

Button cheeped in reply.

"I know you're trying to help," said Jasmine, "and I wish I could understand you. I haven't had a single good idea. I was going to paint stones as paperweights, but Tom said Zara's doing that. I tried weaving a basket, but it looked like a two-year-old had done it. I could make a collage, I suppose, but it's not very exciting. I just can't think of anything original."

The door that separated the barn from the milking parlor slid along its runners. Jasmine looked up to see her father in the doorway. The parlor wasn't used for milking anymore, as Dad

only kept beef cows, but it had running water, so they still used the sink and taps.

"That old ewe didn't last the night, I'm afraid," Dad said.

"Oh, no," said Jasmine. "The one who lambed yesterday?"

"Yes. I thought she wouldn't make it. It's a shame, poor old thing."

"How's the lamb?"

"Pretty weak. She's under that lamp." He pointed to a pen at the other end of the row.

With Button in the palm of her hand, Jasmine climbed out of his pen and went to look at the tiny ewe lamb. She lay shivering in the corner of her pen, her eyes closed.

"I've given her colostrum through a stomach tube," said Dad. "Hopefully that will perk her up a bit. You can try her with some milk in a bit."

"You poor little thing," said Jasmine. "Look, Button, this little lamb is an orphan, just like you. She'll be lonely, too."

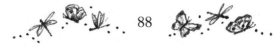

88

Suddenly, an idea popped into Jasmine's head.

"Can we move her into the empty pen next to Button? It's got a heat lamp, too, and I'll be out here all the time, so I can feed her and keep her company."

"Good idea," said Dad. "Bed it down and bring her across. I need to see to the calves."

"Betty," said Jasmine.

"What?"

"That's what I'm going to call the lamb."

"Oh, right." Dad left the barn.

Jasmine reached into the pen and stroked the lamb's soft, nubbly wool. She could feel the ribs under her skin as she shivered.

"Don't worry, Betty," she said. "I'll look after you. And you'll have Button in the next pen to keep you company. Everything's going to be all right."

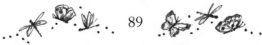

10
We Have to Look After Her

Jasmine put Button back in his own pen. She pulled her scissors from her coat pocket and cut a doorway into the side of his box.

"There. Now you can go in and out whenever you like. You can explore the whole pen."

She climbed out, grabbed an armful of straw from the opened bale at the side of the barn, and shook it over the floor of the empty pen next door.

She walked over to the pen at the other end of

the row, where Betty was lying, her eyes closed, her breathing fast and shallow. Gently, Jasmine lifted her up, carried her to the pen next to Button's, and placed her under the heat lamp.

"There you are, Betty," she said. "That will be nice and warm for you. And I'm going to be here all day, looking after you."

The lamb lay on her side under the lamp, her legs straight out in front of her. Her skinny ribs moved up and down under her thin coat. Jasmine's heart went out to the poor motherless creature. Imagine being one day old and completely alone in the world.

Jasmine sat on the straw next to the lamb, stroking her and speaking gently, but Betty's eyes stayed closed and she didn't move.

Button ran, cheeping, across his pen toward Jasmine. He tripped and fell on his face in the straw, but he got back onto his big webbed feet immediately and started running again. He poked his bill through the chicken wire, cheeping loudly.

"Do you want to come in here with me? Come on, then."

Jasmine leaned over the rail and scooped up the little duckling. She sat him on her lap next to the lamb.

"Betty's very weak and sad at the moment, Button, so we have to look after her."

Button scrambled off Jasmine's lap. He waddled across the straw to the little lamb and walked right over her legs. The lamb didn't move.

"It's a good thing you're so light, Button. I don't have to worry that you'll hurt poor Betty."

Button waddled up to Betty's head. He nibbled gently at the wool on her face.

"Be careful," said Jasmine. "She might not like it."

Button continued to nuzzle the lamb's face all over with his bill. His actions reminded Jasmine of videos she had watched on Mom's computer, where ducklings nibbled and nudged at their newly hatched siblings, apparently trying to encourage them into life.

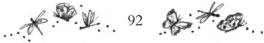 92

"Are you trying to help her?" she asked Button. "Are you trying to wake her up?"

Button seemed to be doing exactly that. He kept nuzzling gently at the motionless lamb, as though trying to revive her.

Jasmine sat still and watched.

After several minutes, Betty's head moved, very slightly, on the straw. Her eyes flickered open and closed again.

Was Button annoying the lamb? Jasmine wondered if she should take him away. But he seemed to like her, and it must be a good thing if she was moving.

Betty lay still as Button waddled around her, nibbling at her wool.

Then, as he nibbled at her face, she opened her eyes. She shifted on her side. Her legs twitched.

"She's trying to get up," Jasmine said. "You clever duck, Button. You've revived her."

The lamb kicked her legs back and heaved herself into a sitting position. She looked at Button,

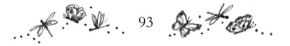

standing in the straw, cheeping at her. Then she craned her neck forward, poked out her tiny pink tongue, and licked the duckling's face.

When, some time later, her father returned to the barn with a packed lunch for Jasmine, he stopped outside Button's pen and laughed in surprise. Jasmine had moved the box into the corner. In the middle of the pen, under the heat lamp, sat a contented-looking lamb. And, snuggled up next to her, huddled into her side, was a fluffy mallard duckling. Jasmine was sitting on a bale of hay in a corner of the pen, drawing them in her sketchbook.

"I tried to put Button back in here," she explained, "but he cheeped and flapped so much, and Betty bleated so much, that I didn't want to separate them. They really wanted to be together. I couldn't leave Button in the other pen, in case a rat got him, so I moved Betty in here. So neither of them will be lonely now, will they? They've

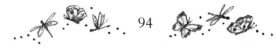

both found a friend. They'll be all right together, won't they?"

"I don't see why not," said Dad. "The only problem would be if the lamb accidentally crushed

him. But as long as you keep an eye on them, they shouldn't come to much harm."

"Tom will help. He's coming over in a minute. I'm hoping he'll give me an idea for my project."

"What project's this, then?"

"You know, the one I told you about. We have to make something from things we've found in nature. Tom's made these amazing wooden animals."

"So what are you making?"

"That's the problem. I have no idea."

Dad smiled at her. "Four weeks ago, you found a clutch of duck eggs by the river. I don't know what you're racking your brain for, Jas. I think your school project is right here in this barn."

11
She's Ruptured My Appendix

"It's so unfair," said Manu. It was the first day back after break and Mom was driving them to school.

"What's unfair?" asked Mom.

"Noah's mom won't let us do fire eating at the talent show."

"Really? That's shocking."

"But we've got another plan."

"What's that, then?"

"Sumo wrestling."

Mom laughed so much she actually snorted.

"But you don't even study sumo wrestling," said Jasmine.

"You don't have to *learn* sumo wrestling. You just wear the outfit and wrestle . . . right?"

"Let me know what your teacher says, won't you," said Mom. "I just wish I could be there when you tell her."

They had reached the school gates now. Mom stopped the car. Jasmine hoisted her schoolbag onto her shoulder and got out slowly and carefully, carrying the big cardboard box as steadily as she could.

"Good luck," said Mom. "Dad will come and collect him at break time."

Tom was waiting at the gate.

"Is he OK?" he asked.

"Yes, he's fine. Let's take him to the office."

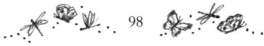

When they explained the situation to Mr. Hampton, he agreed that Jasmine could show her project first.

"Tom's going to grab something from the office while I start," said Jasmine.

She picked up her sketchbook, took an empty paint tray from the back of the classroom, and walked to the front.

"Five weeks ago," she said, "Tom and I found a nest of duck eggs by the riverbank in my dad's sheep field. A dog had killed the mother duck." She shot a look at Bella, who looked away. Nobody in the class knew about Bella's part in the ducklings' story. "We took the eggs to my house and borrowed an incubator."

She showed the class her sketches of the two eggs inside the incubator and explained how it worked. "One duckling, sadly, died just after it hatched, but this is how the last egg turned out."

She nodded at Tom, who was standing outside the door, looking through the glass panel. He came in and gently set the box down on the teacher's desk.

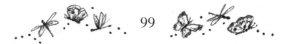

"Everyone needs to be really quiet," Jasmine said, "so you don't frighten him."

The class watched in silent anticipation as she opened the flaps, reached into the box, and lifted out Button.

A hysterical chorus of screeches, oohs, and aahs broke out all around the room. People at the back stood up to get a closer look. There was a babble of talking and questions.

"Oh, that is so cute!"

"Can I hold it? Can I hold it?"

"How old is he?"

"Does he live in your house?"

Button cheeped and flapped in alarm. Jasmine had to cup her other hand over the little duckling to keep him still.

"Shh," hissed Tom, flapping his

hands wildly. "Everyone be quiet. You'll scare him."

The class gradually quieted, and so did the duckling.

"This is Button," said Jasmine. "He's one week old."

"Let's have some questions," said Mr. Hampton.

Hands shot up, faces glowing with excitement. Jasmine was surprised to see that Bella's hand was raised highest of all.

"Bella, you start," said the teacher.

Bella shot a look of triumph at Jasmine.

"She didn't make it."

Mr. Hampton looked taken aback.

"I'm sorry?" he said.

"She didn't *make* that duckling. It just hatched out of an egg. She's cheating."

Mr. Hampton gave Bella a steady look. "Bella, how long would you say it took to make your face cream?"

Bella shrugged. "I don't know. An hour?"

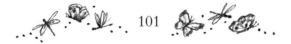

Mr. Hampton turned to Jasmine.

"How long would you say you've spent looking after this duckling?"

"Well, all of vacation, really," said Jasmine. "He needs a lot of food and water, and ducklings are really messy, so I have to clean out his house a lot. And he sees me as his mother, so I spend a lot of time with him. Although he's made friends with an orphaned lamb now, so he doesn't need me around the whole time. Which is lucky, since it's not vacation anymore."

"So," said Mr. Hampton, looking at Bella, "I think you'll agree that Jasmine has, in fact, put a lot of time and effort into making this duckling. Let's have another question."

"Can he fly?" asked Poppy.

"Not until he's a few months old," said Jasmine.

"And then will he fly off?" asked George.

"No. Ducklings treat the first living thing they see as their mother. So Button will always stay near me."

"Can I hold him?" asked Julia.

"That's up to Jasmine," said Mr. Hampton. "What do you think?"

"As long as you're careful," said Jasmine. "He's still really tiny and delicate. Hold him in your palm and cup your other hand gently over him."

"Put your hand up," said Mr. Hampton, "if you'd like a once-in-a-lifetime opportunity to hold a ridiculously cute duckling."

Every single member of the class raised a hand. Some people raised both hands. Even Bella Bradley raised her hand, though she tried her best to look bored and uninterested while doing so.

"Just remember he's a living creature, not a toy," said Mr. Hampton, "and treat him with care and respect."

Jasmine took Button around the room, giving everybody a turn to hold him. She watched anxiously for any signs of distress, but he seemed quite happy in different people's hands. She arrived at Bella's seat. Bella held out her hand.

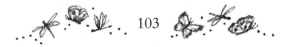

"Be really careful," said Jasmine.

"Obviously," said Bella. "It's not that hard."

Jasmine decided not to respond to that. She placed Button gently in Bella's palm.

"Oh, its feet feel so weird!" squealed Bella. "Ow, they're tickling! Ugh, what's *that*?"

She looked down at her hand and screamed. "Ugh, it pooped on me!"

She jerked her hand away. Jasmine's world went into horrific slow motion as Button was flung into the air. The class gasped as he landed on the floor and lay there, motionless.

Her heart thumping in terror, Jasmine sank to her knees by the tiny body of her duckling. Tom rushed across the room and knelt beside her. Button lay perfectly still, his eyes closed.

He's dead, thought Jasmine. *Button is dead and it's all my fault for bringing him into school and letting people hold him.*

And then Button blinked.

He opened his eyes.

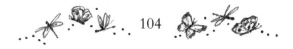

He lifted his head.

He scrambled to his feet.

He staggered forward.

He shook his head.

He walked forward again, more steadily now.

He started cheeping.

Tom picked him up. "I think he's OK," he said.

"Right, that's quite enough drama for one morning," said Mr. Hampton. "Let's put the duckling back in his box."

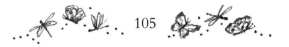

"See," said Bella. "It's fine. No need to fuss."

A switch flicked inside Jasmine. She felt her face heat up and rage rise through her body. She sprang to her feet and towered over Bella's chair.

"You awful, awful brat!" she shouted. "I told you to hold him carefully. I told you to look after him. And you nearly killed him. You killed his mother and now you nearly killed him, you horrible girl."

In a blind fury, Jasmine snatched Bella's jar of face cream from the table, wrenched off the lid, and tipped it onto Bella's head. There was another gasp from the class. Pink gloop oozed all over Bella's hair and started dripping down her face.

Bella jumped up with an outraged cry. She grabbed a handful of Jasmine's hair and yanked it. Jasmine swung her arm back and punched Bella in the stomach.

"That's enough!" said Mr. Hampton. "Stop that right now."

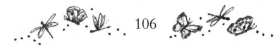

Bella was lying on the floor, clutching her stomach, crying hysterically. "Ow, she's broken my ribs! She's punctuated my liver! She's ruptured my appendix!"

"Good," said Jasmine. "I wish I'd hit you harder."

"That's quite enough from you, Jasmine," said Mr. Hampton. "Go to the principal's office at once. And George, fetch the nurse, please."

Bella writhed and moaned on the floor as Jasmine marched out of the room.

"Did she have to go to the hospital?" asked Manu later.

"No, she was fine, unfortunately. Although she made so much fuss you'd have thought she was dying."

"You should have punched her in the head and knocked her out. I would have."

"Stop that, Manu," said Mom. "I don't want to be called in to see Mrs. Allerton again, thank you."

"Well, she deserved it," said Manu. "Dropping that poor duckling."

"Anyway," said Jasmine, "Mr. Hampton's put us at different tables now. So it was worth it."

"What did the principal say?" asked Ella.

"All the things you'd expect a principal to say," said Mom. "But somehow I got the feeling that, in her heart of hearts, she had a little bit of sympathy for Jasmine."

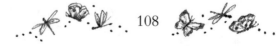

12
Smoke!

"You can turn the tap off now," called Jasmine.

The water in the hose slowed to a trickle and Tom emerged from the milking parlor.

Jasmine propped a short plank against the side of the pool and kissed the top of Button's head. "Let's see if he likes it."

It was the first Saturday of spring vacation. Jasmine and Tom had enlarged Button's pen and blown up Jasmine's old inflatable pool to put in one corner.

"It's way better than the baby bathtub," said Tom. "He'll be able to actually swim in here. And Betty likes it, too."

Betty had grown strong and healthy in the last few weeks, due in great part, Jasmine was sure, to her friendship with Button, from whom she was inseparable. Now Betty stood at the edge of the pool, wiggling her tail and sucking up the water.

Button, who at eight weeks old was almost fully feathered, inspected the ramp, walking around it and jabbing at it with his bill. It seemed to meet with his approval, because he stepped onto the plank and waddled up it. At the top, he paused for a second, then plopped into the water and started to swim, bobbing up and down, pedaling his big webbed feet.

Jasmine tossed a handful of torn-up lettuce leaves into the pool. Button darted around, gobbling up the greens as he swam.

From the barn doorway, where his leash was tied to a post, Jake barked.

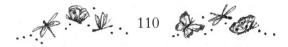

"He wants to round up the sheep," said Tom.

Jake did seem desperate to round up the sheep. There weren't many left in the barn now, just the youngest and weakest lambs and their mothers, plus Betty, of course, and a little one who had caught a chill in the rain a few days earlier and had a hacking cough. Jake watched them all constantly, following their movements with his eyes, his body alert and twitching.

Jasmine walked over and stroked him.

"These sheep don't need rounding up, Jake. We'll go for a nice walk instead. We'll just put Betty back in her own pen first."

"Sorry, Betty," said Tom as he lifted the wriggling, bleating lamb into her own pen. "I know you hate being separated from Button, but you can't swim like him, and we don't want you to fall in and drown."

They took Jake for a long walk in the woods and made their way back through the fields, the collie wagging his tail and sniffing excitedly in

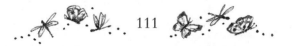

the hedgerows. As they came through a field of cows, Jasmine waved to her dad, who was mending the fence on the other side.

"Do you want lunch?" she asked Tom when they reached the yard. "Mom's at work, but there are pizzas we can heat up. Manu's at Ben's, so we can have a whole one each."

Tom stopped and frowned.

"Listen."

Jasmine listened.

"Button!"

The quacking came from the direction of the barn. But it was not Button's usual quiet, contented quacking. It was loud, urgent, and panicked.

"A fox!" cried Jasmine. "Oh no! I didn't put the netting on the pen!"

She raced toward the barn. *Oh, please, please,* she thought, *let Button be safe.*

At that moment, the duckling came running across the yard toward her, flapping his wings and squawking in distress.

"Button!" cried Jasmine. "How did you get out? What's going on? Is there a fox?"

She bent down to pick him up, but Button flapped his wings as if to bat her hands away, jabbed his bill frantically at her boots, and started running back toward the barn, still squawking. After a few seconds, he stopped and looked back at Jasmine, who was standing still, frowning in bewilderment. Button waddled back to her, grabbed a piece of her pant leg in his bill, and tugged at it urgently.

"He wants you to follow him," said Tom.

The children ran toward the barn, only stopping to tie Jake's leash to a gatepost. As they drew

closer, Jasmine smelled something that made her stomach churn.

"Smoke!"

They came to a dead stop in the doorway.

Orange flames covered the floor of Button's pen. Jasmine stared, frozen with horror, as the flames licked and crackled their way across the barn. The ewes and lambs bolted around their pens in panic, baaing and bleating, butting at the rails. And Button ran into the barn to peck frantically at the rails of Betty's pen as Betty bleated and threw herself at the bars.

In a flash, Jasmine saw that Betty's pen was protected from the fire by Button's paddling pool. But not for long. One side of the pool was already beginning to melt. Would it burst into flames any minute?

Tom and Jasmine both sprang into action at the same moment. They rushed across the barn. Jasmine felt burning heat on her skin. Smoke filled her nose and ash blew into her

114

eyes, making them smart and water. Tom seized Button and Jasmine climbed into Betty's pen. She grabbed the bleating, kicking lamb and handed her to Tom, who had Button under his other arm.

"Take them away," she shouted, clambering over the fence into the next pen. "I'll get this one."

Tom ran out of the barn. Her eyes streaming from the smoke and ash, Jasmine grabbed the sick lamb, climbed out, and ran out of the barn with him. Tom, coughing, his eyes red and watering, raced back in to free a ewe and twin lambs from the next pen.

"I'll do the last two," Jasmine shouted. "You phone the fire department. And my dad."

Tom drove the ewe and lambs into the yard and pulled his phone from his pocket. Jasmine ran back into the barn. The flames were spreading faster now. She must get these sheep out quickly.

The mothers were frantic with worry, baaing and stamping, ramming the rails with their heads. Jasmine slipped off the loop of baler twine that fastened the gate on the next pen. She pulled the gate open and the ewes and lambs bolted out. Jasmine shooed them out to the yard. She did the same with the sheep in the final pen. Mad with fright, they scattered in all directions.

What if they ran back into the barn?

Suddenly, a flash of black-and-white fur raced into the yard.

Jake!

 116

Jasmine didn't know what to do. Jake was her responsibility and she mustn't put him in danger. She should call him and tie him up again.

But he wouldn't be in danger as long as he stayed in the yard, and he clearly just wanted to round up the sheep. He was doing a good job, too, running around the edges of the scattered little flock, gradually herding them into a tight group in the middle of the yard.

She looked back into the barn. The flames were devouring the straw in the sheep pens. Thank goodness the sheep were safe.

But what about the calves in the next barn? How could she stop the fire from spreading?

Of course!

She ran into the milking parlor, where the hose was still connected to the tap. She wrenched the tap around as far as it would go, dragged the hose into the barn, and started spraying water on the dry straw at the edges of the fire.

"The fire department's coming," shouted Tom

from behind her. "And your dad and mom. Hose the wall, too."

He was pointing to the wall that divided the lambing barn from the calves' barn.

Jasmine thrust the hose at him. "You do that. I'm going to let the calves out."

She turned to run, but something banged against her leg. She looked down.

It was Betty. She must have broken free from the group. In a blind panic, she was running straight toward the fire.

"No!" Jasmine shouted. "Betty, come back!"

She started to race after the lamb, but Tom grabbed her around the middle and pulled her back. She struggled, but he was stronger than he looked.

"Let go!" she shouted. "I have to get her out!"

"Don't even think about it!" yelled Tom.

"I have to! Do you want her to die? Oh, no, no!"

Because there, waddling, squawking, and flapping toward the fire after the lamb, was Button.

"No!" screamed Jasmine. "Tom, let me go! I have to get them!"

But Tom wouldn't let go, and Button was almost invisible now in the smoke. Betty was nowhere to be seen. Jasmine tried to call them, but the smoke got in her mouth and all she could do was wheeze and cough. She struggled against Tom but she couldn't break free.

Suddenly, a blur of black-and-white shot past them.

Jasmine's heart froze. Now Jake was going to die, too. She couldn't bear it.

She tried to wrench herself free, but Tom only tightened his grip. And then, through the din of crackling straw, roaring flames, and distressed animals, she heard the rumble of an engine.

She turned to see Dad jumping down from his tractor cab and racing toward them, faster than she had ever seen him move. He picked her and Tom up, one under each arm, like sacks of feed, and ran into the yard, where he dumped

them on the ground and wrenched the hose from Jasmine's grip.

"Get back!" he yelled.

And then Jasmine glimpsed a faint white blur. It was Betty, stumbling out of the dense black smoke. Behind her came Jake. In his mouth he carried the little, limp body of a duck.

13

Cleverer Than the Average Duck

"Get away from the fire!" shouted Dad over his shoulder as he ran to the calves' barn. "Go indoors!"

But before Tom could stop her, Jasmine raced to Jake.

"Sit, Jake," she said.

Jake sat, still holding the duck in his mouth. Jasmine dropped to her knees in front of him and cradled Button's soft, unmoving body.

"Drop him," she said to Jake.

Jake opened his mouth and let go of Button.

"Good dog," said Jasmine. She stood up, with Button in her arms. And Button shook his head and opened his eyes.

"He's awake!" she said. "Oh, Button, I was so worried about you!"

Beside her, Tom was holding Betty, who was coughing and wheezing.

"We need to get them treated," said Jasmine. "Urgently. They definitely inhaled smoke."

She heard tires splashing through puddles, and into the yard came Mom's muddy old station wagon. Jasmine had never been so pleased to see it.

Mom stopped the car beside the children and opened the door. "Oh, thank goodness you're all right," she said, flinging her arms around Jasmine and Tom.

"Careful," said Jasmine, disentangling herself. "You'll hurt Button. He needs treating. And Betty."

"Where's Dad?" asked Mom. "He's not in the barn, is he?"

"He's getting the calves out," said Jasmine, pointing toward the field next to the calves' barn, where the calves were now gathering.

"Oh, thank goodness," said Mom again. Jasmine

thought she was talking about the calves, but then she saw Mom was looking in the opposite direction. Two fire engines were bumping up the farm road.

"Can you examine Button and Betty?" said Jasmine. "They ran into the burning barn and Jake rescued them, so he needs checking, too."

Dad appeared from the calves' barn as the fire engines rumbled into the yard.

"Will you be all right," Mom asked Dad, "if I look at these animals?"

"Sure," he said, pointing the firefighters in the direction of the barn. The engines turned around the corner of the yard.

"Right," said Mom to Jasmine and Tom. "Take them into the cowshed and I'll examine them properly."

Jasmine and Tom carried Button and Betty into the cowshed, which was the building farthest away from the barns, and sat on a bale. Mom came in, carrying a big plastic crate of medicine.

"I'm going to look at Button first," she said, kneeling in front of him, "since birds' airways and lungs are extremely sensitive, so he's probably the most affected. Although none of them looks too bad, really, considering what they've been through. Sit them on the bales and fetch a dish of fresh water for each of them, would you?"

When Jasmine and Tom returned with the water, Mom was examining Button. Jasmine put the dish in front of him. He stretched out his neck, dipped his beak in the dish, and started slurping the water. Betty and Jake drank theirs, too.

"That's a very good sign, that he can drink unaided," said Mom. "Excellent." She reached into her medicine box and took out what looked like an asthma inhaler. "Now, unfortunately, there can often be delayed pulmonary irritation—that's lung damage—even if there are no obvious external injuries. How long were they exposed to the smoke?"

"Not that long," said Jasmine. "Button escaped and warned us about the fire when it must have only just started."

Mom looked quizzically at Jasmine. "He warned you about the fire?"

"Yes, he came running across the yard and tugged at Jas's pants to tell her to follow him," said Tom.

"Wow," said Mom. "That's a pretty special duck you've got there, Jasmine."

"I know," said Jasmine, stroking his silky feathers.

"But I thought you said something about them running into the burning barn?"

"They did," said Tom. "Betty must have panicked or something and she ran back into the barn, and then Button ran in after her."

"I'm sure he was trying to tell her to get out," said Jasmine.

"And then Jake ran in and brought them both out," said Tom.

"What a hero," said Mom, stroking Jake. "Thank goodness they all got out safely. And well done, you two, for having the sense not to run in after them."

Jasmine's and Tom's eyes met briefly over Mom's head.

"I'm going to give Button a bronchodilator and an anti-inflammatory through the inhaler," said Mom. "You hold him on your lap, Jasmine, while I administer it. This will help keep his airways clear." She puffed the inhaler into the air around Button's face. "I'll give some to Betty and Jake, too. And I'm going to give them all a broad-spectrum antibiotic, to prevent secondary infections. We'll need to keep a close eye on them for a couple of weeks, to check for delayed reactions."

"Shall we keep Betty and Button in here together?" asked Jasmine.

"Yes, that would be ideal," said Mom. "It's nice and peaceful, and they won't be disturbed. Button will need a bath to wash the toxins from his feathers. You can bring the baby bathtub out here. They'll need a lot of fresh drinking water, and we must be alert for any signs of breathing problems. But I think they'll be OK."

She stroked the duck's feathers. "Well done,

Button, for warning Jasmine about the fire so quickly."

When Dad came in twenty minutes later, Button was already waddling around the cowshed, exploring his new surroundings.

"Here they are," said Dad, smiling at Jasmine and Tom. "The heroes of the hour. The firefighters couldn't stop singing your praises. Massively impressed, they were, that you had the presence of mind to hose the walls."

"You hosed the walls?" said Mom, frowning. "You didn't go into the barn, did you?"

"Didn't they tell you?" said Dad. "They brought all the sheep and lambs out."

Mom's face went rigid as she stared at Jasmine. "You did *what*?"

"Well, who did you think got the sheep out?" said Dad.

"I thought you did, of course."

"I was down in the Thirteen Acres. By the time

I got here, these two had already done it. I just rounded them up and put them in the field."

Seeing the look on Mom's face, Jasmine changed the subject. "Have they put the fire out now?" she asked Dad.

Dad nodded. "All done, thank goodness. And all the animals saved, thanks to you two."

"I can't believe you ran into a burning barn," said Mom. "You could have been killed."

"But if we hadn't done it," said Jasmine, "the sheep would have been killed. And we're fine, aren't we?"

Mom shook her head in despair as they heard a car coming up the driveway. "That will be Ben's mom with Manu," she said, and went into the yard.

"Do they know how the fire started?" Tom asked Dad.

"They think the heat lamp in Button's pen set fire to the straw. They found the lamp on the ground. Probably a rat chewed through the cable."

Jasmine shivered. "Thank goodness Button got out. He'd have been burned to death."

Ella appeared in the doorway, a book in her hand. "Why are there fire engines here?" she asked. "Has something happened?"

Running footsteps sounded outside and Manu pushed past Ella into the cowshed.

"I can't believe I missed it. It's so unfair. The one exciting thing that's happened in my whole life and I wasn't here. And now they've put the fire out and ruined it all. Ben's really angry, too."

"The fire engines are still here," said Dad. "If you're lucky, they might let you have a look inside."

Manu's face lit up. "Cool!" He rushed out the door. "Ben! Come and see the fire engines!"

Button flapped up onto Jasmine's lap. She laid her cheek against his silky feathers. They smelled of smoke.

"I reckon he's cleverer than the average duck, that mallard," said Dad.

"He's the real hero," said Jasmine. "If he hadn't escaped and warned me and Tom, we wouldn't have known about the fire until it was too late." She shuddered. "Imagine, those poor, poor sheep."

"He's had a lot of adventures," said Tom, "considering he's not even fully grown yet."

Jasmine counted on her fingers. "Orphaned on the nest, the only survivor out of nine eggs, made friends with a lamb, got thrown on the floor by Bella Bradley, saved the sheep from a fire, and ran into a burning barn to rescue his friend."

"I think that's quite enough excitement for one young duck," said Dad. "A quiet life for you from now on, eh, Button?"

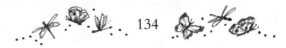

Jasmine smiled at Button. He looked at her and gently nibbled her hair.

"Oh, I think Button will have plenty more adventures in the future," Jasmine said. "I can't wait to see what he does next."

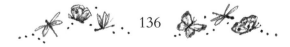

Turn the page for
an interview with Jasmine and
a sneak peek of the next book in the
JASMINE GREEN RESCUES series!

A Q&A with Jasmine Green

What do you have in an animal rescue kit?

It's always useful to carry a bottle of water. You can use it to clean wounds and also give the animal a drink if it's dehydrated. If you find a sick or injured animal, the best thing to do is to keep it warm and take it to a vet or a wildlife rescue organization. I'm lucky because my mom is a vet! If you need to look after an animal yourself, you could keep some rehydration mix in your house, and also animal feeding bottles with teats of different sizes. A syringe is good, too. If an animal is too weak to suck from a bottle, you can drip the formula into the side of its mouth with the syringe. It's good to have a supply of cardboard boxes, where a sick animal can be kept safe and warm, and some old towels to use for bedding. A heating pad or hot water bottle is useful, too, as sick or injured animals need to be kept warm. But every animal is different, so you'll need to ask an expert on the best way to care for any animal you find. The internet is really helpful for finding people in your neighborhood with experience looking after different animals. Ask an adult to help!

How can I help animals in my neighborhood?

The best thing to do is to make sure your neighborhood is as animal-friendly as possible. If you see litter lying around, pick it up and dispose of it safely. Animals can get caught up in netting or suffocate in plastic bags. If you have a yard, keep part of it wildlife-friendly, with long grass, wildflowers, and undergrowth where birds, butterflies, insects, and small mammals can flourish. Perhaps you could have a birdbath or hang up bird feeders where wild birds can come and feed. And if you're able to have a pond, they are wonderful wildlife habitats.

How many animals do you have now?

I have my two cats, Toffee and Marmite, my pig, Truffle, and now Button the duck! He's a mallard drake, and he's extremely handsome. His mother was a wild duck, but I hatched Button in an incubator and I was the first person he saw when he hatched, so he thought I was his mom! That meant he was too tame to go back and live in the wild, so now he lives on the farm with my dad's chickens. Sometimes I think Button believes he's the king of the chickens!

Jasmine Green Rescues
Rescues
A Collie
Called Sky

1

A Tiny Whimper

Jasmine and her best friend, Tom, were shoveling pig feed into a bucket when Jasmine suddenly remembered something.

"Guess what?" she said. "I'm going to be looking after two chinchillas in August."

Tom's eyes lit up. "Oh, chinchillas are so cute! Whose are they?"

Jasmine picked up the bucket. "They belong to one of the other vets at Mom's office," she said as they crossed the farmyard toward the orchard.

"They're called Clover and Daisy. They've got this huge cage that's going to go in my bedroom. I can't wait."

A large mallard drake waddled across the yard toward them, flapping his wings and quacking. Jasmine laughed as he nibbled at her boots.

"Don't be jealous, Button," she said, stroking his silky feathers. "You know you're the best duck in the whole world. And Clover and Daisy are only coming for two weeks. You're mine forever."

Tom and Jasmine had rescued Button in the spring, when he was just an orphaned egg on the riverbank. Button's name suited him because his perfectly round eyes looked like two shiny black buttons. He was a fully grown drake now, living happily with the chickens, but he still liked to follow Jasmine around the farmyard and be petted.

"Are you getting paid to look after the chinchillas?" asked Tom.

"I don't know. If I do, I'll need to give the money to Dad for Truffle's feed. She eats so much these days. But that's the whole point of having animals to board, isn't it—so that we have enough money to look after rescued animals."

The two friends were planning to set up an animal rescue and boarding center when they grew up. The idea had been inspired by Truffle, Jasmine's pet pig, who was now trotting across the orchard to greet them. She had been a tiny runt piglet on the point of death when Jasmine had smuggled her home from a neighboring farm and nursed her back to health eight months ago.

Tom tipped the feed into Truffle's trough, and Jasmine scratched her behind the ears as she gobbled the pignuts.

"When are the chinchillas coming?" asked Tom.

"Not until the middle of August. Three weeks to go."

When Tom had to go home for lunch, Jasmine walked up the farm driveway with him. Fluffy white clouds perched high in the bright-blue sky.

"The sky looks like a painting, doesn't it?" said Jasmine.

"It's better than a painting," said Tom, "because it changes all the time."

"Like a new painting every day."

In the field to the left of the driveway, Jasmine spotted her five-year-old brother, Manu, and his best friend, Ben, crouched by a clump of hawthorn bushes.

"Look what we found!" called Manu.

"Ugh," said Tom. "That's creepy."

It was an animal's skull, with big eye sockets and a complete set of teeth.

"Look, it still works," said Ben. He moved the lower jaw to make the mouth open and shut.

"It's a badger," said Manu. "We've got a leg bone, too. We're looking for the rest of it."

"I'm hungry," said Ben.

"There's cookies at home," said Manu, and they ambled back toward the house.

Jasmine said goodbye to Tom at the end of

the driveway. As she turned to walk back home, a little sound made her stop. Frowning in concentration, she stood still and listened.

The air hummed with insects. Bees buzzed in the clover and butterflies fluttered among the dog roses and rosebay willowherb. In the next field, a kestrel hovered, waiting to pounce on its prey.

I must have imagined it, she thought. She started to walk on. But then she heard it again. A tiny whimper. It seemed to be coming from the hedge.

Jasmine walked back and scanned the thick hedgerow. There was no sign of an animal. She dropped to her knees and looked underneath the hedge.

And then she saw something. A heap of matted black and white fur. Was it a dead animal? A badger, perhaps?

The heap of fur whimpered again. Jasmine moved closer so she could see it properly.

A dog! A little border collie, hardly more than a puppy, by the looks of it. But it wasn't a normal, healthy puppy. It looked barely alive. Its eyes were closed and its bones jutted out beneath the dull, matted fur.

"Hello," said Jasmine softly. "Hello, little dog. What are you doing under there?"

The puppy whimpered again, but it didn't move.

"Are you hurt?" Jasmine asked. "Are you stuck? Let me get you out of there."

She reached in and gently put her arms around the little dog. She picked it up and gasped in shock. It was much lighter than she had expected. Its hip and shoulder bones stuck out from its body, and she could see every one of its ribs under the matted coat.

"Oh, my goodness," she said. "Oh, you poor, poor thing, you're starving!"

The puppy lay limp in Jasmine's arms, taking fast, shallow breaths. She tried to stand it up but it just flopped down again on its side in the grass.

It clearly had no strength at all in its legs. It didn't even seem to be able to lift its head up.

Jasmine looked at her watch. Her mom, who was a vet, would still be taking morning clients at the practice where she worked, four miles away. Jasmine could call her and ask her to bring medicines and supplies, but she wouldn't be able to get back for at least an hour. Dad had gone to collect some new beef calves from a neighboring farm. Jasmine's older sister, Ella, was at home, but she wouldn't have a clue what to do with a sick puppy.

Jasmine scooped the little dog up in her arms and held it close. The puppy opened its amber eyes and looked at her, and the tip of its tail slowly began to wag. The look in its eyes was one of absolute trust.

Jasmine bent down and kissed the top of its head.

"Don't worry, little dog," she said. "I'm going to take you home and make you better. You'll be all right now. I promise."

Which animals have you helped Jasmine rescue?

- ☐ A Piglet Called Truffle
- ☐ A Duckling Called Button
- ☐ A Collie Called Sky
- ☐ A Kitten Called Holly
- ☐ A Lamb Called Lucky
- ☐ A Goat Called Willow

About the Creators

Helen Peters is the author of numerous books for young readers that feature heroic girls saving the day on farms. She grew up on an old-fashioned farm in England, surrounded by family, animals, and mud. Helen Peters lives in London.

Ellie Snowdon is a children's author-illustrator from a tiny village in South Wales. She received her MA in children's book illustration at Cambridge School of Art. Ellie Snowdon lives in Cambridge, England.

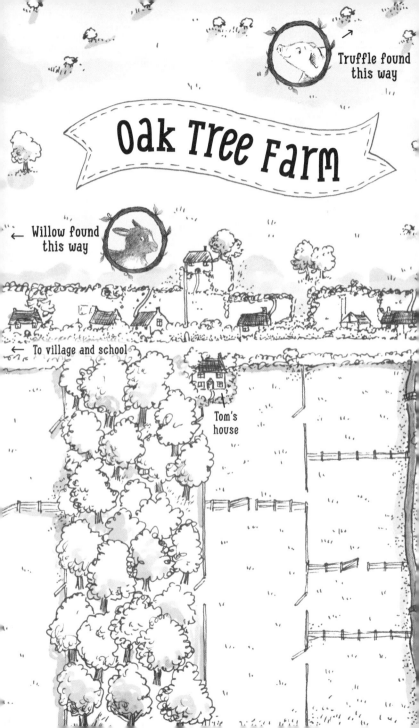

Oak Tree Farm

Truffle found
this way

Willow found
this way

← To village and school

Tom's
house